I LOVE YOU, LITTLE MONSTER

Giles Andreae   Jess Mikhail

ORCHARD

One evening, long after my sleep time
Big softly crept to my bed
And stretched out warm fingers to ruffle my hair
"I love you, my darling," Big said.

For Freya, with love
G.A.

For Mum and Dad
J.M.

ORCHARD BOOKS
338 Euston Road, London NW1 3BH
Orchard Books Australia
Level 17/207 Kent Street, Sydney, NSW 2000

First published in 2006 as *Keep Love In Your Heart, Little One* by Orchard Books
First published in paperback in 2011 as *I Love You, Little Monster* by Orchard Books
This edition published in 2012

A CIP catalogue record for this book is available from the British Library.

ISBN 978 1 40831 427 2

1 3 5 7 9 10 8 6 4 2

Printed in China

Orchard Books is a division of Hachette Children's Books,
an Hachette UK company.
www.hachette.co.uk

Now, Big must have thought I was sleeping
And I didn't open an eye.
Instead I just let the words float through my mind
Like balloons floating up through the sky.

"I love you, my Small," Big continued
"But there's so much to do in the day
That it's hard to sit down and to make enough time
To say all of the things I should say.

"And it's funny, but now that you're sleeping
And everything's quiet and calm
The words seem to be much more easy to speak."
And Big laid a soft hand on my arm.

"You're everything I always dreamed of
You've got so much beauty inside
The way that you smile, that you laugh, that you dance
Makes my heart want to sing out with pride.

"You live as though life's one huge present
Unwrapping a bit every day
That's just how we all should be living, my love
And look at you showing the way!

"And sometimes I know when I scold you
You feel that I'm being unfair
But please understand that it's just out of love,"
And Big swept back a strand of my hair.

"There are things in this life that can hurt you
They come to us all – that I know.
But they all give us chances to learn, darling Small
And they all give us chances to grow.

"So when you get knocked down, my sweetheart
Look up at the sky without fear
For sometimes we need to be flat on our backs
Before starlight begins to appear.

"And please, above all else remember
Keep love in your heart, little one
Reach out to the world like a beautiful flower
Stretches out to the warmth of the sun.

"It's the only sure way to be happy
The only sure way to be free.
Believe in yourself and believe in your dreams
And you'll be what you dream you can be."

With that, Big lay down on my pillow
And planted a kiss on my head.
"My beautiful, wonderful, glorious child
You light up my world," Big then said.

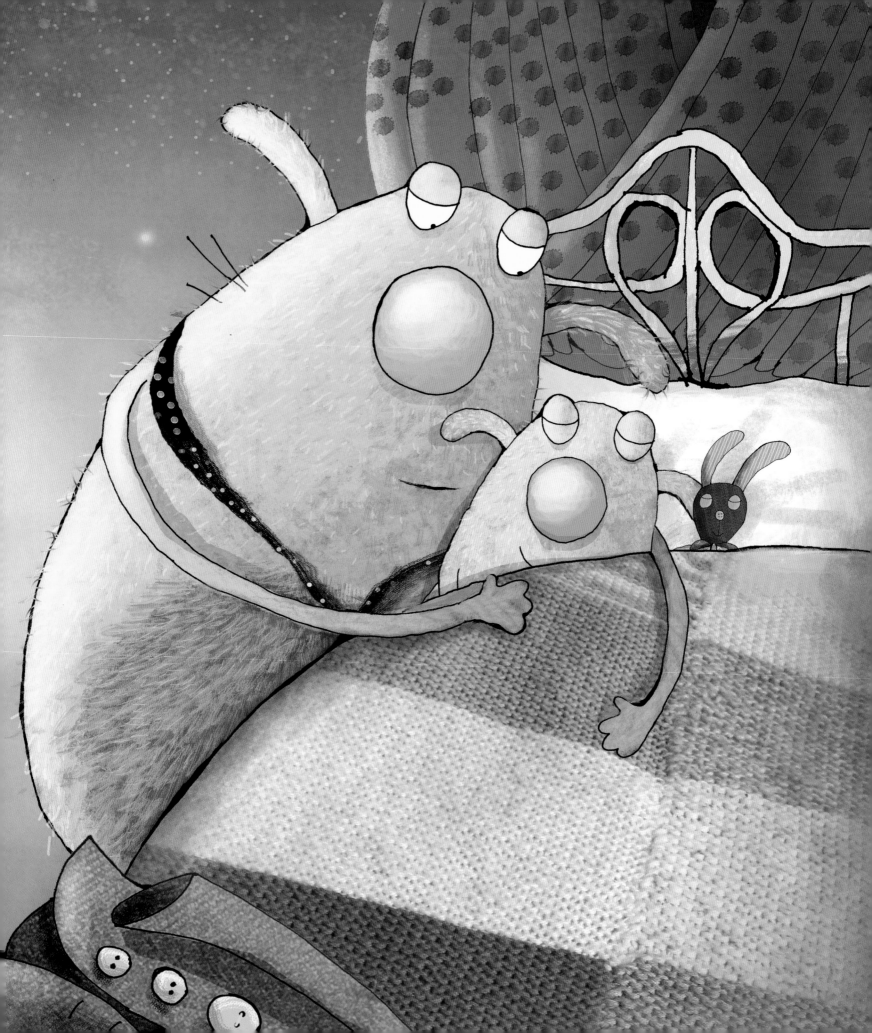

With that, Big crept out of my bedroom
Turning round for one last little peep.
I hugged my small pillow and smiled a big smile
And then slowly I drifted to sleep.

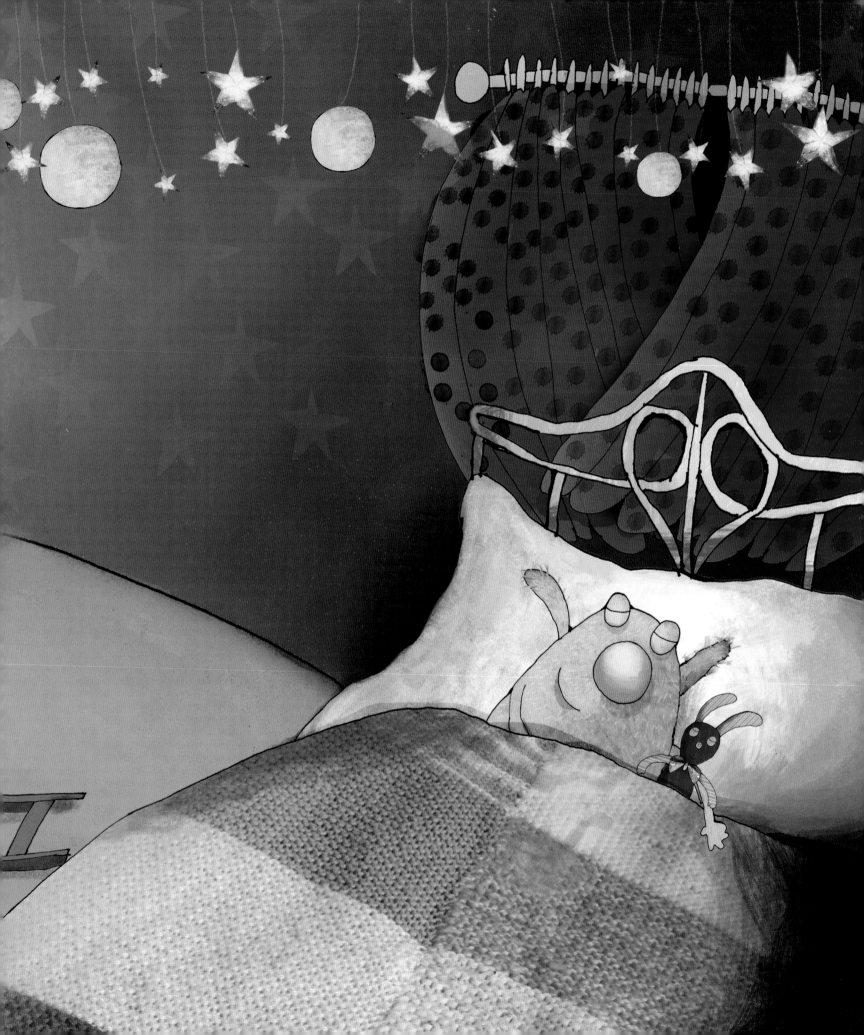